W9-BSJ-318

Colette

Fifi

On the third day of Christmas a mademoiselle from Paris sent her true love three French hens, two turtledoves, and a partridge in a pear tree.

The hens never arrived.

By MARGIE PALATINI

Illustrations by RICHARD EGIELSKI

HYPERION BOOKS FOR CHILDREN *New York*

Three French Hens

A HOLIDAY TALE

In the unclaimed mail department
of the New York City Post Office . . .

Since the hens were mailed off during a Paris drizzle, the address on their package ended up smudged. Yes, not a word could be read. And somehow, some way, the ladies became, shall we say, misdirected.

Alas . . . undeliverable.

However, Colette, Poulette, and Fifi were not about to be left languishing as unclaimed mail when they had a true love to make happy. No, no!

After all . . . this was Christmas! And they were French!

"We will deliver ourselves!" declared the trio.

Yet, as determined as any three French hens could be, how were they to find this *Monsieur Philippe Renard*?

"Of course! Ze phone book!" proclaimed Colette.

Poulette flipped and flapped through page after page. Sadly, there was not a Philippe Renard to be found. All still looked lost (including the hens), and then . . .

"Zis is New York, not Paree!" exclaimed Fifi. "We must translate! It is not Philippe Renard, but Phil Fox who we must see!"

And so the three French hens dusted themselves off, picked themselves up, and headed down into the subway in search of Mr. Phil Fox.

Meanwhile, somewhere in New York City...

Down on his luck, Phil Fox was staring out his window with no view. He did not have a true love. He did not even have a friend. (Unless he counted the cockroach.) Why, the poor fellow hadn't had a square meal in a month.

These were lean times for Phil. Very lean times.

As he watched the first snowflakes of the season fall, he made a wish.

Phil looked over to the cockroach and shrugged. "Hey, my luck's just gotta change pretty soon, right? 'Tis the season."

Suddenly, there was a knock on the door.

"Bonjour! Merry Christmas! *Joyeux Noël*, Monsieur Philippe Renard!" sang out the three French hens. "We are Colette, Poulette, and Fifi! A present from your true love!"

Now, Phil knew all well and good that he was not Philippe Renard. He was very sure he wasn't anyone's true love. And he barely knew a word of French.

But . . . Phil was a clever enough fox to recognize a free meal when he saw one. Three French hens on his doorstep? It was better than Chinese takeout.

"Well, well, well," gulped Phil.

"Pouvons-nous entrer?" asked the hens.

"Entrée? Entrée! Most definitely entrée!" he answered with a grin as his roast, fry, and sauté walked through the door.

Before Phil could get out his cookbook, Colette whisked the fox into the *salle de bain*.

"*Pour vous*—for you, Monsieur Philippe," she clucked, showing him a tub filled with perfumed bubbles.

A bath had been foreign to Phil in the past. But if it was good enough for *Philippe*, Phil thought he'd give it a go.

The water was warm and wonderful. The fragrance heavenly.

Phil sniffed. He soaked. He sighed. He knew . . .

There was no way he could have Colette for breakfast.

Most certainly not after she'd given him a manicure, a new coiffure, and dressed him in such dandy new attire.

He looked so swell. Swank. Dare he say it? *Debonair!*

The new, natty Phil looked in the mirror. He looked at the beaming Colette. Phil sighed and smiled wistfully. . . . He was definitely going to have to skip breakfast.

But when Poulette called from the other room . . .

Foxy Phil was ready for lunch.

"*Voilà*, Monsieur Philippe!" declared Poulette with a flourish.

Phil could not believe his eyes. His space was no longer shabby, but chic!

And standing tall in the corner was the most beautiful twinkling tinseled tree.
"I am a wonder with ze needle, thread, and evergreen! *Oui?*" Poulette said proudly.

"Yes! *Oui, oui!*" agreed Phil as the tasteful hen ushered him to a big stuffed chair by the crackling fire. She plumped and poofed him a pillow. Slid a tuffet under his slippered toes.

Phil felt so warm. So comfy. So cozy. So—*not* able to have Poulette for lunch. Not even for hors d'oeuvres.

However, though Phil may have felt toasty and looked swanky, his tummy was still cranky. When it began to grumble loudly, Phil's thoughts wandered to hen number three.

Oh, yes. Mr. Fox was planning dinner with Fifi.

"*Bon appétit*, Monsieur Philippe!" shouted Chef Fifi as she came through the swinging kitchen door. She held a tray high with canapés, consommés, hollandaise, and patés.

She had salades niçoises and bowls of vichyssoise. Parfaits. Crème brûlée.
Chocolate mousse. Charlotte russe.

Phil sniffed. Tasted. Nibbled. Noshed.

He looked at the three hens and the tower of French food and thought . . . Eh? So who needs chicken?

He delicately wiped his chin with a monogrammed napkin. Now, *that's* what he called a breakfast, lunch, and dinner. With style, too.

Yes, Phil was feeling very happy. And full. He was also feeling something else. And it wasn't indigestion.

Phil was so filled with holiday spirit (and a guilty conscience) that he finally confessed.

"Ladies. I gotta get this off my chest. I'm not who you think I am! I'm a fake!" cried Phil. "A phony! Hey—I'm *faux*! I'm not even French!"

The hens huddled. Clucked. Concluded. "Zat does not matter."

"But . . . I don't have a true love," continued Phil. "Not even a friend. It's only me and the cockroach. I don't even get kissed under mistletoe."

"Zat does not matter," the three hens repeated.

Phil hung his head and gulped with guilt. "You don't understand. I am not Philippe Renard from Paree. I'm just plain ol' Phil Fox from the Bronx."

"Zat does not matter," the trio trilled. "We like you just ze way you are—*notre ami*—our friend, Phil."

"Friend?" Phil felt a lump in his throat. Even the cockroach had a tear in his eye.

Phil never thought he would have such fine friends. Certainly not feathered ones. How could he ever repay their kindness?

Then Phil looked under his twinkling tree. There were so many presents. Too many for just one simple fox. What the heck, thought Phil. It's Christmas! He would share his good fortune and holiday cheer with his new friends.

He handed Colette, Poulette, and Fifi three of his beautifully wrapped presents.

The hens smiled, but shook their heads. "What's wrong?" asked Phil.

"Thank you, *merci*, dear friend, Phil," said Fifi. "But we cannot accept zeez gifts for *Christmas*."

"But why not?" asked a bewildered Phil.

Poulette smiled. "Because . . . our holiday is Hanukkah. We're kosher chickens."

Phil grinned and gave a hearty hug to each. "No matter! I say, Happy Holidays to us all!"

This could be the beginning of a beautiful friendship.

And so, the three French hens from Paris and Phil Fox from the Bronx celebrated the rest of the twelve days of Christmas, *and* eight nights of Hanukkah together.

And they all had a wonderful time.

Including the cockroach.

FIN

(The End)

Text copyright © 2005 by Margie Palatini
Illustrations copyright © 2005 by Richard Egielski

All rights reserved. No part of this book may be reproduced or transmitted in any form or by any means, electronic or mechanical, including photocopying, recording, or by any information storage and retrieval system, without written permission from the publisher. For information address Hyperion Books for Children, 114 Fifth Avenue, New York, New York 10011-5690.

Printed in Singapore
First Edition
3 5 7 9 10 8 6 4 2
This book is set in Colwell.
Reinforced binding
ISBN 0-7868-5167-8
Library of Congress Cataloging-in-Publication Data on file.
Visit www.hyperionbooksforchildren.com